HELICOPTERS

PHYLLIS EMERT

WILD WINGS

JULIAN Ⓜ MESSNER

The author wishes to acknowledge the Carruthers Aviation Collection, Sprague Library, Harvey Mudd College, Claremont, California, and express thanks to Nancy R. Waldman, Librarian, Sprague Library, for her help and cooperation in preparation of the *Wild Wings* series.

The Agusta A 109A MK II is an Italian-made helicopter. All others in the book are American in origin.

JULIAN MESSNER and colophon are trademarks of Simon & Schuster, Inc.
Manufactured in the United States of America.

Lib. ed. 10 9 8 7 6 5 4 3 2 1
Paper ed. 10 9 8 7 6 5 4 3 2 1

Library of Congress Cataloging-in-Publication Data

Emert, Phyllis Raybin.
    Helicopters / Phyllis Emert.
        p.   cm. – (Wild wings)
    Includes bibliographical references.
    Summary: Describes the specifications and uses of various kinds of helicopters, including the Boeing Vertol CH-47D Chinook, the Bell AH-1G Hueycobra, and the McDonnell Douglas AH-64 Apache.
    1. Helicopters—Juvenile literature.   [1. Helicopters.]
I. Title.   II. Series: Emert, Phyllis Raybin.   Wild wings.
TL716.E48   1990
629.133'352—dc20
    ISBN 0-671-68962-2 (lib. bdg.)   ISBN 0-671-68967-3 (pbk.)
                                                90-31573
                                                CIP
                                                AC

Photo credits and acknowledgments

Pages 14, 17, 34, and 37 courtesy of Kaman
Pages 18, 21, 26, 29, 42, and 45 courtesy of Bell
Pages 22 and 25 courtesy of Boeing
Pages 30, 33, 38, 41, 54, and 57 courtesy of Sikorsky
Pages 46, 49, 58, and 61 courtesy of McDonnell Douglas

CONTENTS

INTRODUCTION

The helicopter is valuable because it can do many things that other aircraft can't do. It can take off and land vertically in very small spaces. It can hover in one spot in midair without moving. It can even move backward or from side to side.

A helicopter can reach places once thought unreachable and it doesn't need a path, a road, a field, or a runway. It can fly to high mountaintops or isolated arctic areas. It can land on ships, in the jungle, or on water. It can lift tons of equipment and other aircraft. It can save lives by flying the injured to nearby hospitals quickly. It can destroy enemy tanks and ships.

Helicopters are used in search and rescue, as troop and supply transports, as passenger shuttles, and as heavy-lift flying cranes. They're used in firefighting, police patrol, crop dusting, and mail delivery. They're also used as attack aircraft and gunships.

Igor Sikorsky, a famous builder of helicopters, once called them "the most universal vehicles ever created and used by man."

BELL 47
1940s–Early 1970s

SPECIFICATIONS

ENGINE:
Number: 1
Manufacturer: Franklin
Model: 6V4-178-B32 6-cylinder
Rating: 178 horsepower

ACCOMMODATIONS:
Seating for 3 passengers and for 2 wounded in stretchers carried outside pilot's compartment with special attachment

DIMENSIONS:
Diameter of Main Rotor: 35 feet, 1½ inches
Length: 41 feet, 4¾ inches
Height: 9 feet, 2 inches

OTHER INFORMATION:
Manufacturer: Bell
Crew: 3
Maximum Takeoff Weight: About 2,000 pounds
Ceiling: 14,500 feet
Maximum Range: 214 miles
Maximum Speed: 92 miles per hour

The Bell 47 was the first helicopter in the world to be approved for commercial production by the United States government. From 1946 to 1973, thousands of 47 models were used in more than 40 countries around the world. Different versions were built for a variety of jobs.

The Bell 47 was easily recognized by its bubble-type see-through Plexiglas canopy. It had an open tail section which showed the criss-cross metal structure of the helicopter and its engine. The six-cylinder, 178-horsepower Franklin engine allowed the Bell 47 to reach speeds of up to 92 miles per hour.

Its twin-blade rotor was more than 35 feet in diameter. The clop-clop sound it made resulted in the nickname "chopper," which became a term for all helicopters.

Many Bell 47s were used in rescue and evacuation work by the military in the Korean War (1950–1953). This was the first combat situation in which helicopters played a major role. They were fitted with special aluminum stretcher containers mounted on each landing skid to carry out the wounded. Plexiglas windscreens protected the patient's head and shoulders.

Without helicopters, it took 10 to 14 hours to transport wounded soldiers to field hospitals. Many died before they ever got help. Bell 47 medevac (medical evacuation) helicopters could fly wounded troops to hospital units within an hour. Some dedicated pilots even flew at night to rescue soldiers. They read the dials and gauges in the cockpit with a flashlight.

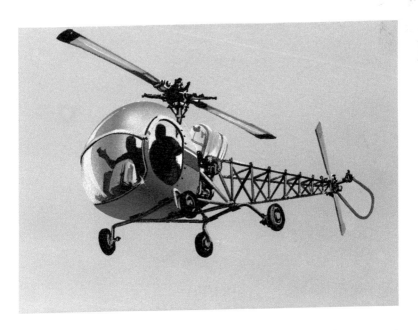

Bell 47s were also used to carry survey crews to isolated or hard-to-reach areas. Some were equipped with flotation gear for working over water or swamps. Others were used to lay telephone cables and power lines, and to fight forest fires. Many were used in agriculture to dust and spray crops for weed and pest control.

The Bell 47 was one of the most widely built and popular helicopters of all time. Sixty different versions were built in Great Britain, Italy, and Japan, as well as in the United States.

SIKORSKY H-34 CHOCTAW
1950s–1980s

SPECIFICATIONS

ENGINE:
Number: 1
Manufacturer: Wright
Model: R-1820-84 B/D 9-cylinder
Rating: 1,525 horsepower

ACCOMMODATIONS:
• 16 to 18 troops
        or
• 8 stretcher patients

DIMENSIONS:
Diameter of Main Rotor: 56 feet
Length: 56 feet, 8¼ inches
Height: 15 feet, 11 inches

OTHER INFORMATION:
Manufacturer: Sikorsky
Crew: 2
Maximum Takeoff Weight: 14,000 pounds
Ceiling: 9,500 feet
Maximum Range: 247 miles
Maximum Speed: 122 miles per hour

The H-34 Choctaw was one of many versions of Sikorsky's S-58 model helicopters, which were among the most successful ever produced. It was first used as a troop transport and general-purpose helicopter by the United States Army in 1955. It could carry 16 to 18 soldiers, or eight patients in stretchers. The Army also used the H-34 as a crane helicopter to lift and transport heavy loads.

The Navy's version was used in antisubmarine patrol work. It operated from cruisers or aircraft carriers at sea as a search-and-attack chopper carrying weapons. Some Choctaws were fitted with special sonar search equipment which could be lowered into the ocean to locate hidden enemy subs.

Marine versions were used as general transport helicopters. A few were assigned special duty with the United States space programs and recovered satellites that returned to earth.

The Choctaw's 1,525-horsepower Wright engine was mounted in the nose of the helicopter. The pilot's compartment seated two, and was located above and slightly in front of the cabin.

A nine-cylinder piston engine powered the main rotor of the H-34, which has four blades and is 56 feet in diameter. When the pilot gives the blades the correct pitch angle, the whirling rotors create lift. Without pitch, helicopters won't rise.

The main rotor produces torque. This is a twisting motion that swings the helicopter around. To control torque, helicopters have tail rotors which revolve at right angles to the main rotor.

The tail rotor also controls the direction of flight. The pilot uses rudder pedals to turn the chopper left or right by changing the pitch of the tail rotor. The Choctaw's tail rotor has four blades and is nine feet, six inches in diameter.

Different versions of the H-34 were used by more than a dozen countries throughout the world. A 12-seat model was operated by several airlines to carry civilian passengers.

After 1970, Sikorsky sold special kits to convert piston-engined Choctaws to gas turbine propulsion. This extended the life of the helicopter, and some are still used today in civilian and military service.

KAMAN H-43B HUSKIE
1950s–1970s

SPECIFICATIONS

ENGINE:
Number: 1
Manufacturer: Lycoming (Ly-KOH-ming)
Model: T53-L-1B turboshaft
Rating: 825 horsepower

ACCOMMODATIONS:
• 2 firefighters and 1,000 pounds of firefighting and rescue gear
  or
• up to 8 passengers
  or
• 4 stretcher patients and medical attendant

DIMENSIONS:
Diameter of Rotors: 47 feet each
Length: 25 feet, 2 inches
Height: 15 feet, 6½ inches

OTHER INFORMATION:
Manufacturer: Kaman (KAY-men)
Crew: 1–2
Maximum Takeoff Weight: 9,150 pounds
Ceiling: 25,000 feet
Maximum Range: 277 miles
Maximum Speed: 120 miles per hour

The Kaman H-43 Huskie was a crash and rescue helicopter used by the United States Navy and Air Force. It first flew in the 1950s during the Korean War.

The H-43A model was powered by a piston engine and had two rotors which tilted outward from the top of the helicopter. The rotors revolved in opposite directions from each other and were each 47 feet in diameter. Each overcame the other's natural torque (turning or twisting), so a tail rotor wasn't necessary. Instead, the tail unit had twin rudders which controlled the direction of flight.

The H-43B version, which first flew in 1956, was powered by one 825-horsepower turboshaft engine. It had twice the cabin space and double the payload of the 43A. It carried two firefighters and 1,000 pounds of firefighting and rescue equipment, or up to eight passengers, or four stretcher patients and a medical attendant. Many 43B Huskies were used at United States Air Force bases throughout the world.

The more powerful H-43F model, which seated 11 passengers, was built in 1964. It was designed for hot day/high altitude conditions. The 43B and 43F Huskies were used in the Vietnam War as rescue helicopters.

A typical mission in Vietnam began with an emergency radio message. "We've got a C-130 transport down in the jungle with a crew of four. Proceed immediately five miles northwest of your present location."

"We're on our way," declared the Huskie pilot.

The rescue copter flew at top speed (120 miles per hour) to the crash site. Within minutes the pilot saw the big transport plane in flames in a jungle clearing. He maneuvered the chopper close to what was left of the C-130. The downwash of air from the two rotors beat back the flames.

"There's movement down there," shouted the pilot. "Let's smother the fire and get the crew out."

Two firefighters onboard the Huskie released more than 60 gallons of fire retardant carried underneath the fuselage. The chemicals put out what was left of the fire.

The copter set down in the clearing close to the smoldering transport. Huskie crew members raced to the wreckage and discovered two people with minor burns and injuries. They searched further into the debris.

"We've got two major injury cases here. Looks like severe burns and a possible broken back. Get the stretchers!"

Once the injured were settled in the Huskie, it flew them to a military hospital for treatment. The plane was a loss but all four of the crew survived.

H-43 Huskie crash and rescue helicopters saved the lives of hundreds of aircraft crews whose planes crashed and burned in peace and in wartime.

BELL UH-1B HUEY
1950s–1980s

SPECIFICATIONS

ENGINE:
Number: 1
Manufacturer: Lycoming
Model: T-53-L-11 turboshaft
Rating: 1,100 horsepower

ACCOMMODATIONS:
• 7 troops
      or
• 3 stretchers and 2 sitting wounded and attendant
      or
• 3,000 pounds of freight

FIREPOWER:
• 40mm grenade launcher
      or
• 4 7.62mm M-60 machine guns and 2.75-inch rockets

DIMENSIONS:
Diameter of Main Rotor: 44 feet
Length: 42 feet, 7 inches
Height: 14 feet, 7 inches

OTHER INFORMATION:
Manufacturer: Bell
Crew: 2
Maximum Takeoff Weight: 8,500 pounds
Ceiling: 16,700 feet
Maximum Range: 212 miles
Maximum Speed: 138 miles per hour

The Bell UH-1 Iroquois, nicknamed "Huey," was the most widely used and well-known helicopter series in the Vietnam War. During the 1960s and into the 1970s, thousands of Hueys performed a variety of jobs in the jungles of Southeast Asia.

First flown in 1956, the UH-1 was originally designed as a light utility, training, and casualty evacuation (casevac) copter. Many were used as troop transports, flying soldiers directly into areas of battle. But the Hueys were unarmed and the helicopter and its troops were open to enemy fire.

In the early 1960s, this problem was solved by fitting the UH-1B model with M-60 machine guns, rockets, and grenade launchers. These Huey gunships acted as escorts to troop transports.

A typical mission began at dawn. A group of 10 choppers flew high over the jungle and rice paddies to a clearing in enemy territory. The Huey gunships dove down and sprayed the landing zone with long bursts of machine-gun and rocket fire. The hidden enemy fought back with rifles and machine guns of their own.

Huey troop transports moved in fast and touched down. Soldiers leaped from the copters, ran into the high grass and took up battle positions. Gunners stood at the open cabin door of the helicopters and fired their rifles at the enemy to protect the troops.

The Huey gunships continued this suppressive fire. They kept the enemy busy while their own troops took cover and the empty transports flew away. Rockets exploded in the surrounding jungle. Grenades were launched. Bullets flew through the air. Round after round was fired until the transports climbed to safer altitudes.

The Hueys returned later in the day and picked up the soldiers who survived the mission. The wounded were

flown to rear field hospitals. One of the choppers was disabled by enemy fire. The crew left it there and flew back in another copter.

The UH-1 Huey was the main battlefield support helicopter in Vietnam. For countless soldiers, it was the difference between life and death. The use of Huey gunships in Vietnam paved the way for the later development of American attack helicopters.

In a period of 20 years, Bell produced more than 12,000 UH-1 helicopters in a dozen different models. Later versions were heavier, more powerful, and carried up to 14 troops or six stretcher patients and a medical attendant.

UH-1 models were also manufactured in Italy, Germany, and Japan and are still used today by dozens of countries throughout the world.

BOEING VERTOL CH-47D CHINOOK

1960s–1980s and beyond

SPECIFICATIONS

ENGINE:
Number: 2
Manufacturer: Avco Lycoming
Model: T55-L-712 turboshafts
Rating: 3,750 horsepower each

ACCOMMODATIONS:
• 33 to 44 troops
     or
• 24 stretcher patients and 2 attendants
     or
• Maximum payload of 28,000 pounds carried inside
  cabin or on outside cargo hooks

DIMENSIONS:
Diameter of Rotors: 60 feet each
Length: 99 feet
Height: 18 feet, 7/8 inch

OTHER INFORMATION:
Manufacturer: Boeing Vertol (BOH-ing VER-tol)
Crew: 2–3
Maximum Takeoff Weight: 50,000 pounds
Ceiling: 14,000 feet, depending on load
Maximum Range: 230 miles
Maximum Speed: About 185 miles per hour

The Boeing Vertol CH-47D Chinook is a medium-lift twin-rotor transport helicopter in use today by more than a dozen countries worldwide. The CH-47D models are expected to be operational into the next century.

The first Chinook flew in 1961. It was designed to transport troops and cargo under difficult and varied altitudes and temperatures. About 600 CH-47As, Bs, and Cs were used by the United States Army in the Vietnam War in the late 1960s and early 1970s. The models differed from each other in engine power and performance.

In Vietnam, Chinooks landed combat-ready troops in the middle of enemy territory. A ramp at the back of the fuselage lowered to allow soldiers to get out quickly and cargo to be unloaded. If the jungle was too thick for the copter to land, the troops climbed down rope ladders while the Chinook hovered in the air.

The twin-engined helicopter flew light artillery, ammunition, and other supplies and equipment to the battlefield. The cargo was carried inside the cabin or underneath the body on cargo hooks.

Chinooks were also used in aircraft recovery and casualty evacuation. They retrieved more than 11,000 aircraft, worth millions of dollars, which had been shot down or disabled in Vietnam.

The Chinook fuselage was shaped like a large box. The cabin was seven and half feet wide, six and a half feet high, and over 30 feet long. It carried 44 fully equipped troops or 24 stretcher patients and two attendants.

The CH-47 could set down on water as well as on land. It had a watertight fuselage and special pods along its sides to help keep it afloat.

In the 1980s, early model Chinooks were rebuilt into CH-47Ds. Their engines were replaced with two more-powerful T55-L-712 turboshaft engines with 3,750 horse-

power each. The rotor transmission was replaced and the flight deck redesigned. The electrical, hydraulic, flight control and avionics (aviation electronics) systems were all improved and modernized.

The CH-47D has more than double the payload of the CH-47A and a 100 percent increase in performance. It can carry the Army's new 155mm howitzer, as well as its 11-man crew, a total load of 22,000 pounds. The CH-47D is the only Army helicopter capable of lifting the 24,750-pound D5 bulldozer.

Great Britain, Canada, Australia, Japan, Italy, Argentina, Spain, Thailand, and Morocco, among others, use Chinook transport helicopters in their armed forces.

BELL 206 JETRANGER
1960s – 1980s and beyond

SPECIFICATIONS

ENGINE:
Number: 1
Manufacturer: Allison
Model: 250-C20 turboshaft
Rating: 400 horsepower

ACCOMMODATIONS:
Up to 5 people, with up to 250 pounds of baggage in a separate compartment; outside cargo sling can carry 1,200 pounds

DIMENSIONS:
Diameter of Main Rotor: 33 feet, 4 inches
Length: 38 feet, 9½ inches
Height: 9 feet, 6½ inches

OTHER INFORMATION:
Manufacturer: Bell
Crew: 1 or more
Maximum Takeoff Weight: 3,200 pounds
Ceiling: 20,000 feet
Maximum Range: 388 miles
Maximum Speed: 140 miles per hour

The Bell 206 JetRanger, first flown in 1962, is one of the most successful light, general-purpose civil helicopters. New and improved versions of the JetRanger are used today as air taxis, in business and industry, and by law enforcement and government agencies.

This small, speedy helicopter can fly up to 140 miles per hour over a range of nearly 400 miles. The JetRanger is designed for high performance under hot day/high altitude conditions.

The United States Army version is the OH-58A Kiowa. It's used by the armed forces of over two dozen countries throughout the world.

JetRangers have several nonmilitary uses. They service and supply offshore oil drilling platforms in the Gulf of Mexico and off the northeastern and western coasts of the United States. They fly relief crews, other personnel, supplies, tools, and equipment to oil rigs which otherwise could only be reached by boat.

JetRangers are also used by police to patrol highways, observe driving conditions, and report on traffic problems. They've been used in fighting forest fires—a large bucket attachment carried under the fuselage is filled with lake water and dumped directly onto the blaze. Some have pop-out floats which allow the copter to land on water in emergencies.

Many JetRangers have been used in rescue work and in natural disasters such as hurricanes and earthquakes. Their ability to hover in the air allows them to reach areas where other vehicles can't go. One actually landed on the overturned hull of a capsized oil tanker. A welder cut a hole in the ship's bottom to free trapped crewmen.

In disaster situations, when roads are blocked and airport runways are damaged, helicopters have proven

themselves invaluable in providing assistance and transportation to those in need.

In the Southern California earthquake of 1971, power and telephone lines came down. Overpasses fell onto freeways below. Buildings collapsed and 64 people were killed. Traffic and communications came to a stop.

Within minutes of the quake, helicopters all over the stricken city were in the air. Many were Bell JetRangers used by the Los Angeles police, city, and county fire departments and the county sheriff's office.

The Veterans Hospital in Sylmar was completely demolished. JetRangers picked up the injured and flew them to other hospitals 50 to 60 miles away. The copters also flew in doctors and medical supplies.

One JetRanger, equipped for live television coverage, broadcast disaster news to all the major networks. Others helped in the evacuation of people from damaged buildings and dangerous areas.

Helicopters were also used in the San Francisco earthquake of 1989.

SIKORSKY 2-64 SKYCRANE

1960s–1980s

SPECIFICATIONS

ENGINE:
Number: 2
Manufacturer: Pratt and Whitney
Model: JFTD12A-1 turboshaft
Rating: 4,050 horsepower each

ACCOMMODATIONS:
3 crewmembers in cockpit, and payload of 20,000
pounds in containers (pods) fitted underneath boom or
attached to hoist

DIMENSIONS:
Diameter of Main Rotor: 72 feet
Length: 88 feet, 6 inches
Height: 25 feet, 5 inches

OTHER INFORMATION:
Manufacturer: Sikorsky
Crew: 3
Maximum Takeoff Weight: 38,000 pounds
Ceiling: 10,500 feet
Maximum Range: About 200 miles
Maximum Speed: 117 miles per hour

The Sikorsky S-64 Skycrane helicopter could lift and carry loads of up to 20,000 pounds at speeds of more than 100 miles per hour. First flown in 1962, this flying crane had a six-bladed main rotor which was 72 feet in diameter.

There was no fuselage on the Skycrane. Instead, the 88½-foot-long narrow boom connected the rounded cockpit with the four-bladed tail rotor. It also supported the two Pratt and Whitney 4,050-horsepower engines, mounted side-by-side, and the landing gear.

The pilot and copilot sat in the front of the cockpit. A third crewmember sat in a rear-facing seat with a separate set of controls. He could take over the helicopter during loading and unloading.

Containers (called pods) could be attached underneath the boom and lifted for transport. There was more than nine feet of clearance between the boom and the ground to accommodate large, heavy loads. The landing gear could also be lengthened or shortened so the S-64 could crouch over the load and lift it.

The United States Army version of the Skycrane was the CH-54 Tarhe. Many were assigned to the 1st Air Cavalry Division during the Vietnam War. Tarhes recovered over 380 downed American aircraft from behind enemy lines.

Some military pods contained complete mobile field hospitals which were flown to battlefield areas. Other loads were suspended by a cable from a removable 15,000-pound hoist and sling attachment. Tarhes carried bulldozers, gunboats, jeeps, and trucks.

The giant helicopter could transport 48 wounded soldiers in stretchers, or 67 combat-equipped troops in special passenger pods. Once, an Army Tarhe lifted 87 combat soldiers at one time! Another unloaded 304 tons of cargo, usually a three-day job, in four hours and 34 minutes.

Often described as a huge dragonfly, the civilian Sky-crane also transported fresh-cut timber. By flying it directly to the mill, helicopters eliminated the need to build expensive roads to logging stations. The S-62 was used in construction work and carried equipment and even fresh concrete to job sites.

KAMAN SH-2F SEASPRITE
1960s –1990s

SPECIFICATIONS

ENGINE:
Number: 1
Manufacturer: General Electric
Model: T58-GE-8F turboshaft
Rating: 1,350 horsepower

ACCOMMODATIONS:
• 1 passenger (or stretcher patient) with Light Airborne
  Multi-Purpose System (LAMPS) equipment
        or
• 4 passengers
        or
• 2 stretcher patients with sonabuoy launcher removed

FIREPOWER:
• Anti-Submarine Warfare (ASW) homing torpedoes

DIMENSIONS:
Diameter of Main Rotor: 44 feet
Length: 52 feet, 7 inches
Height: 15 feet, 6 inches

OTHER INFORMATION:
Manufacturer: Kaman
Crew: 3
Maximum Takeoff Weight: 13,300 pounds
Ceiling: 22,500 feet
Maximum Range: 422 miles
Maximum Speed: 165 miles per hour

The Kaman SH-2F Seasprite is the United States Navy's standard helicopter for small ships. It is used in Anti-Submarine Warfare (ASW) and Anti-Ship Surveillance and Targeting (ASST) operations, as well as search-and-rescue missions.

The first version of the Seasprite was flown in 1959. This single-turboshaft-engine copter replaced piston-engine helicopters in reconnaissance, supply, casualty evacuation, and rescue missions. Early models carried up to 11 people or four stretcher patients.

The Seasprite had a watertight body for landings at sea. Its floating hull made direct pickups possible from the water in air-sea rescue operations. If the ocean was choppy and the waves were high, the Seasprite used a hoist or heavy cable to pull a downed flyer or sailor up into the copter.

In 1967, Kaman changed its Seasprite helicopters to twin-engined machines. They fitted the copter with two General Electric turboshaft engines, one on each side of the main rotor. This resulted in better performance and gave the copter the ability to carry heavier loads.

Since 1970, the Seasprites have undergone further change. The Navy equipped the helicopters to be used in its Light Airborne Multi-Purpose System (LAMPS) antisubmarine and antimissile defense programs. The version used today is the SH-2F, which has a high-power surface-search radar system and advanced sensor and weapons systems.

The Seasprite is equipped with sonabuoys, which are floating sonar detectors. When dropped in the water they

can accurately pinpoint the location of submerged submarines. They do this by registering the vibrations of high-frequency sound waves in the water.

Mk 44 or Mk 46 ASW homing torpedoes (which lock on to the target) are carried on each side of the copter's fuselage for attacking enemy vessels. They're also equipped with marine flares and smoke markers.

The four-bladed main rotor is 44 feet in diameter and extremely quiet. The speedy Seasprite can fly at 165 miles per hour with a range of over 400 miles.

Squadrons of LAMPS SH-2F helicopters serve on Navy destroyers, frigates, and cruisers in the Mediterranean and the Pacific Ocean. They're expected to be operational into the 1990s.

SIKORSKY CH-53A SEA STALLION
1960s–1980s

SPECIFICATIONS

ENGINE:
Number: 2
Manufacturer: General Electric
Model: T64-GE-6 turboshafts
Rating: 2,850 horsepower each

ACCOMMODATIONS:
• 38 combat-equipped troops
                or
• 24 stretcher patients and 4 attendants
                or
• Normal payload of 8,000 pounds of cargo

DIMENSIONS:
Diameter of Main Rotor: 72 feet
Length: 88 feet, 1½ inches
Height: 24 feet, 11 inches

OTHER INFORMATION:
Manufacturer: Sikorsky
Crew: 3
Maximum Takeoff Weight: About 35,000 pounds
Ceiling: 16,700 feet
Maximum Range: 280 miles
Maximum Speed: 195 miles per hour

The Sikorsky CH-53A Sea Stallion was a heavy assault transport helicopter used by the United States Marine Corps. First flown in 1964, it had a flat-bottomed, fully watertight hull and operated from the deck of aircraft carriers.

When not in use, the six-bladed main rotor (which was 72 feet in diameter) and four-bladed tail rotor were folded automatically by push-button control. This allowed many Sea Stallions to fit onboard the carriers without taking up too much space.

A full-size door and loading ramp in the back end of the Sea Stallion permitted easy loading and unloading of cargo or troops. The 30-foot long cabin accommodated 38 combat-equipped corpsmen or 24 stretcher patients and four attendants. The seats folded up against the walls so the Sea Stallion could be quickly changed from a troop to a cargo transport.

A typical cargo load included two jeeps, two Hawk missiles with control consoles, or a 105mm howitzer. An under-fuselage hook carried loads of up to 8,000 pounds. It lifted and transported airplanes and other large equipment.

The Sea Stallion saw action with the Marines in South Vietnam in the 1960s and 1970s. A Navy version towed magnetic minesweepers in the harbors off the Vietnamese coast. Once a mine was detected, it was blown up without harming boats or people.

The Air Force version had a more powerful engine and a rescue hoist, and was able to be refueled in flight. Many were equipped with three machine guns. The Sea Stallion was also used as a rescue and recovery helicopter for the Apollo manned spacecraft program.

Thirty-five Sea Stallions took part in the largest civilian rescue mission in history. It happened on April 29 and 30,

1975, in Vietnam. Saigon, the capital city of South Vietnam, was about to be overrun by the North Vietnamese Communist forces. The city was in a panic. Mobs roamed the streets. Buildings burned.

Thousands of frantic people gathered at the American Embassy compound. They waited to be airlifted by American helicopters before the Communists entered the city. Many were Vietnamese, along with remaining United States citizens and their families. Scores of helicopters took part in the rescue called " Operation Frequent Wind."

As people were airlifted to the Navy's 7th Fleet, dozens of helicopters were ditched overboard into the sea to make room on deck for more people and incoming copters. Over 590 missions were flown and more than 7,000 people were evacuated to safety aboard American ships.

BELL AH-1G HUEYCOBRA
1960s–1990s

SPECIFICATIONS

ENGINE:
Number: 1
Manufacturer: Lycoming
Model: T53-L-13 turboshaft
Rating: 1,100 horsepower

FIREPOWER:
• 7.62mm minigun in undernose turret
     or
• 2 miniguns
     or
• 2.40mm grenade launchers
     or
• 1 minigun and 1 grenade launcher plus 76 2.75-inch
  rockets mounted on stub-wings
     or
• 28 rockets
     or
• 20mm cannon

DIMENSIONS:
Diameter of Main Rotor: 44 feet
Length: 52 feet, 11½ inches
Height: 13 feet, 5½ inches

OTHER INFORMATION:
Manufacturer: Bell
Crew: 2
Maximum Takeoff Weight: 9,500 pounds
Ceiling: 11,400 feet
Maximum Range: 357 miles
Maximum Speed: 219 miles per hour

43

The Bell AH-1 HueyCobra was the first American heli-copter designed and built as a heavily armed gunship and attack aircraft. Originally flown in 1965, the HueyCobra was equipped with the same engine, transmission, and rotor systems as the UH-1 Huey. But similarities stop there.

The HueyCobra was small, lean, and fast. Its fuselage was only 38 inches wide, five feet narrower than the UH-1 Huey. Flying under the cover of jungle trees, it was a more difficult target for the enemy to spot.

The pilot and gunner sat in tandem, one behind the other, in the fighter-style cockpit. The gunner sat in the front seat and the pilot in the back seat, both protected by armor-plated panels.

The AH-1G carried a wide variety of firepower. A 7.62mm minigun with 8,000 rounds was housed in the un-dernose turret. Some had two miniguns (4,000 rounds each) or two 40mm grenade launchers. Others had one minigun and one grenade launcher.

The HueyCobra had short stub-wings on each side of the fuselage on which were mounted up to 76 2.75-inch rockets in four launchers. Some had 28 rockets or two miniguns or a 20mm cannon. Usually the gunner con-trolled and fired the turret armament and the pilot fired the wing weapons.

The HueyCobra wide-bladed rotor gave it a top speed of 219 miles per hour, nearly 100 mph faster than the UH-1. It was more maneuverable and could carry almost three times the firepower of the Huey. The Cobra could reach its target in half the time, stay twice as long in combat, and deliver more damage to the enemy!

The AH-1G provided escort services and support cover for troop transports during the Vietnam War beginning in 1967. But it was also used as an attack helicopter.

Cobras and OH-6A Cayuse helicopters acted as hunter/killer teams. The smaller, lighter Cayuse purposely flew low over the jungles and drew enemy fire. Right behind and under cover of the trees, the Cobra would then zoom in and blast the enemy with rocket and cannon fire.

Over the years, other versions of the HueyCobra were built which were more powerful, carried more firepower, and had more advanced avionics. The Sea Cobra was the twin-engined model of the HueyCobra built for the United States Marine Corps.

The AH-1S is the modernized version currently in use by the military. Its engineering features and electronics, radar, and weapons are the most advanced available in aviation today. The AH-1S carries one 20mm cannon, eight TOW (Tube-launched, Optically-tracked, Wire-guided) antitank missiles and 70mm rocket launchers.

Many S model HueyCobras serve with the United States Army in Europe (USAREUR). They operate with NATO (North Atlantic Treaty Organization) forces by patrolling the border between West Germany and Czechoslovakia.

McDONNELL DOUGLAS 500E

1980s and beyond

SPECIFICATIONS

ENGINE:
Number: 1
Manufacturer: Allison
Model: 250-C20B turboshaft
Rating: 420 horsepower

ACCOMMODATIONS:
• 2 passengers in forward seat and 2 to 4 passengers (or
  2 stretcher patients and one attendant) in rear section

DIMENSIONS:
Diameter of Main Rotor: 26 feet, 4 inches
Length: 30 feet, 10 inches
Height: 8 feet, 2 inches

OTHER INFORMATION:
Manufacturer: McDonnell Douglas (formerly Hughes)
Crew: 1–2
Maximum Takeoff Weight: 3,550 pounds
Ceiling: 16,000 feet
Maximum Range: About 300 miles
Maximum Speed: 155 miles per hour

The McDonnell Douglas 500E helicopter is the civilian version of the United States Army's OH-6A Cayuse. First flown in 1982, this small, light copter is maneuverable, fast, and powerful for its size.

The pilot and two passengers sit in a forward bench seat in the cabin. The rear section accommodates two to four passengers or two stretcher patients and one medical attendant. Two doors are located on each side of the cabin. Some models have air conditioning, a baggage compartment, and soundproofing.

Many 500E models are used by law enforcement agencies in cities throughout the United States. These police copters are equipped with 30-million candlepower SX-16 Nightsun searchlights, a siren, emergency services communications systems, and a rescue net. A special four-bladed tail rotor reduces the helicopter's noise level from the ground.

A typical police copter may be used in traffic and crowd control and search, rescue, and pursuit activities.

"Copter 2. Code Red. An escaped inmate from the state prison has been spotted in your area. Proceed immediately to 9th and Main."

The pilot of the police helicopter makes a quick turn, increases speed, and is on his way. As he nears the target area, he switches on the bright searchlight beam. It lights up the deserted business district below as if it were daytime.

The pilot notices several police vehicles converging on the area. Suddenly he spots a darting movement out of the corner of his eye. Immediately he aims the brilliant beam of light on an alley 500 feet below.

For a split second a man is frozen in the solid white light. Then he bolts down the alley.

"I'm in pursuit of suspect in alley between 9th and 11th heading west. Let's cut him off at Main," reports the pilot.

The copter follows from above, keeping the suspect in the searchlight as he runs. The pilot switches on his public address system and speaks into the microphone. "This is the police. You are surrounded. Halt immediately! Put your hands in the air and you will not be harmed."

Just then two police cars drive into view. Four officers, guns in hand, jump out of their cars, and take aim at the man in the alley.

The suspect freezes, hands in the air. The helicopter hovers several hundred feet above him until he is hand-cuffed and led away by the officers.

The McDonnell Douglas 500E helicopter is used today by law enforcement agencies in Washington, D.C., and in California, Georgia, Missouri, Oklahoma, and Florida, among others.

AGUSTA A 109A MK II

1970s–1990s and beyond

SPECIFICATIONS

ENGINE:
Number: 2
Manufacturer: Allison
Model: 250-C20B turboshafts
Rating: 420 horsepower each

ACCOMMODATIONS:
• Up to 7 passengers and 330 pounds of baggage
    or
• 2 stretcher patients and 2 medical attendants
    or
• Up to 2,000 pounds of cargo transported on outside hook

DIMENSIONS:
Diameter of Main Rotor: 36 feet, 1 inch
Length: 42 feet, 9¾ inches
Height: 10 feet, 10 inches

OTHER INFORMATION:
Manufacturer: Agusta (uh-GUHS-tuh)
Crew: 1–2
Maximum Takeoff Weight: 5,732 pounds
Ceiling: 15,000 feet
Maximum Range: 363 miles
Maximum Speed: 193 miles per hour

The Agusta A 109A MK II is a light, general-purpose Italian-made helicopter for both civil and military use. Often described as one of the sleekest and most attractive helicopters ever built, it first flew in Italy in 1971. The A 109A was named Hirundo, which in Italian means swallow, a small, speedy bird.

Powered by two Allison turboshaft engines, this copter flies at speeds close to 200 miles per hour. Unlike other light-duty choppers, it has a retractable landing gear which folds up under the fuselage. The streamlined body helps to reduce drag (air resistance) and increases mileage and fuel economy. A specially designed tail rotor drive shaft eliminates cabin vibration.

Passengers of the A 109A make themselves comfortable in two rows of three seats each. A seventh person can sit on the flight deck to the left of the pilot. The ride is smooth and quiet as passengers watch the traffic below from altitudes of up to 15,000 feet.

In 1985, Agusta introduced a wide-body version of the A 109A. Changing the shape of the fuel tanks and using swelled side panels made the cabin larger. A special VIP (very important person) model seats four to five people with a refreshment and music center. One VIP wide-body is used by the president of Italy and operated by the Italian Air Force.

The A 109A can be changed to an air ambulance within minutes. A special medevac version can accommodate one to two stretcher patients with complete monitoring and intensive-care equipment.

The A 109A is built in several military and naval versions. They're equipped with sliding doors, flotation gear, armored seats, and heavy-duty battery and fuel tanks. Many come with advanced radar and navigation sys-

tems, a rescue hoist, and nonretractable landing gear (it doesn't fold up under the fuselage).

The Aerial Scout model can be armed with a machine gun and two rocket launchers. The Light Attack model comes with antitank missiles and an undernose telescopic sight.

The naval version is used in antisubmarine warfare with homing torpedoes and marine markers. As an antishipping helicopter, the A 109A comes with long-range search radar and air-to-surface wire-guided missiles. Other versions are used by the police for patrol and observation, search and rescue, and firefighting.

The Agusta A 109A MK II is used today by Italy, Portugal, and Argentina, among others.

SIKORSKY UH-60 BLACK HAWK

1970s–1990s and beyond

SPECIFICATIONS

ENGINE:
Number: 2
Manufacturer: General Electric
Model: T700-GE-700 turboshaft
Rating: 1,543 horsepower each

ACCOMMODATIONS:
• 11 troops
        or
• 4 stretcher patients and 3 attendants, 2,640 pounds of cargo (or passengers) inside cabin and up to 8,000 pounds of cargo on hook under fuselage

FIREPOWER:
1–2 M-60 machine guns on either side of fuselage

DIMENSIONS:
Diameter of Main Rotor: 53 feet, 8 inches
Length: 64 feet, 10 inches
Height: 16 feet, 10 inches

OTHER INFORMATION:
Manufacturer: Sikorsky
Crew: 3
Maximum Takeoff Weight: 20,250 pounds
Ceiling: 19,000 feet
Maximum Range: 373 miles, fully loaded
Maximum Speed: 224 miles per hour

The Sikorsky UH-60 Black Hawk has been chosen by the Army as its standard battlefield assault transport helicopter for the 1990s and beyond. First flown in 1974, the UH-60 is a wide helicopter with a large cabin that can carry 11 fully equipped troops and a crew of three.

Eight troop seats can be replaced by four stretcher patients when the Black Hawk is used for medical evacuation. As a heavy-lift aircraft, it can carry up to 8,000 pounds on a cargo hook under the fuselage.

The cockpit crew of a UH-60 is confident, knowing the copter was built to take a lot of punishment and still fly. The rotor system can work for 30 minutes after taking a direct hit from a 23mm shell. Its two crash- and bulletproof fuel tanks can survive a hit by a 12.7mm shell.

Armor-piercing 7.62mm bullets won't bring down a Black Hawk for at least 30 minutes. Both the pilot and co-pilot's seats are protected with armor-plating. The UH-60 also carries one or two M60 machine guns which fire through the doors on either side of the fuselage.

The Black Hawk can be airlifted over long distances. One can fit in a C-130 Hercules transport plane. Six can be carried in a giant C-5 Galaxy to trouble spots all over the world.

Black Hawks have already seen action, in the American invasion of Grenada in October 1983. The communist government of this small Caribbean country and its Cuban advisors were a threat to hundreds of American citizens there. The Organization of Eastern Caribbean States requested military aid from the United States.

UH-60 helicopters transported a small force of United States troops to Grenada. Within a few days, the Grenadian militia and the communist government were overthrown and the Black Hawks safely evacuated all Americans.

One model of the UH-60 is designed to intercept and jam enemy communications with special electronics equipment. Other models being developed and tested include a search-and-rescue copter, and one that carries a variety of weapons such as the Hellfire missile and anti-tank land mines.

The Navy's version of the UH-60 Black Hawk is the SH-60B Seahawk. It will eventually replace all Kaman Seasprites in service today. Seahawks will be the Navy's standard antisubmarine and antiship strike helicopter.

The Seahawk differs from the Black Hawk by having a rotor blade and tail rotor that fold automatically for shipboard stowage. It's also equipped with high-powered radar and two torpedoes, and can be refueled in flight.

McDONNELL DOUGLAS AH-64 APACHE

1980s and beyond

SPECIFICATIONS

ENGINE:
Number: 2
Manufacturer: General Electric
Model: T700-GE-700 turboshafts
Rating: 1,536 horsepower each

FIREPOWER:
• 30mm Chain Gun cannon mounted in underfuselage
 turret and up to 16 Hellfire antitank missiles
       or
• Up to 76 2.75-inch rockets
       or
• Combination of missiles and rockets

DIMENSIONS:
Diameter of Main Rotor: 48 feet
Length: 49 feet, 1½ inches
Height: 13 feet, 10 inches

OTHER INFORMATION:
Manufacturer: McDonnell Douglas (formerly Hughes)
Crew: 2
Maximum Takeoff Weight: 17,650 pounds
Ceiling: 20,500 feet
Maximum Range: 380 miles
Maximum Speed: 235 miles per hour

The McDonnell Douglas AH-64 Apache is America's first advanced attack helicopter. Originally flown in 1975, the Apache entered Army service in the mid-1980s after many years of testing.

It will eventually replace the AH-1 HueyCobra gunships now in use as the Army's main antitank helicopter. The Apache's mission is to stay hidden from the enemy at a distance and destroy tanks with its wide range of advanced weapons and sensors.

The keys to its success are the Target Acquisition and Designation System (TADS) and the Pilot's Night Vision Sensor (PNVS). These systems provide the crew with the ability to detect, recognize, and attack enemy targets from a distance during the day, at night, and in bad weather.

The Apache carries up to 16 Hellfire antitank missiles or up to 76 rockets, or a combination of both. A 30mm Chain Gun automatic cannon is mounted in an under-fuselage turret.

The pilot sits 19 inches above and behind the copilot/gunner in the large transparent cockpit. Armor plating and a plastic blast shield protect the two from high explosives and armor-piercing bullets.

Imagine an Apache attack helicopter on wartime patrol in a heavy rainstorm. The pilot uses the PNVS system to fly the copter.

"TADS has locked on to a squadron of enemy tanks and support vehicles, heading west. Range 2.3 miles."

"Fire missiles when ready," orders the pilot.

The co-pilot launches six of the Apache's Hellfire missiles mounted on its small stub-wings. The missiles are laser-guided and home in on light reflected from the target up to a range of three miles.

"I count at least two direct hits and a lot of damage done. They're returning fire."

As the Apache closes in, the pilot notices small-arms fire from armored vehicles below. He turns his head toward the target, framing it in the look-and-shoot gunsight attached to his helmet display sight system. Then the pilot fires 800 rounds per minute from the automatic cannon. At the same time, the co-pilot launches a dozen 2.75-inch rockets.

"Direct hits on target. But we took a few ourselves," says the pilot. "Let's go back to base and check out the damage."

The Apache has the ability to stay in the air for 30 minutes or more after taking direct hits from enemy weapons. It can withstand rifle-caliber ammunition, 23mm explosive shells, and even high-explosive blasts through the main rotor blade and still return to base in one piece.

The speedy and maneuverable AH-64 Apache is in service with the United States Army in Europe (USAREUR) and operates with NATO (North American Treaty Organization) forces there. It's expected to remain operational into the next century.

GLOSSARY

Artillery—Mounted guns of large caliber, too heavy to carry.

Atomic bomb—An extremely destructive type of bomb unleashing the energy of the atom.

Avionics—Aviation electronics.

Bombardier (bom-bar-DEER)—The person who operates the bomb sight and releases the bombs.

Boom—A projecting beam on an airplane which connects the tail rotor to the main body.

Caliber—The diameter of a bullet; the inside diameter of the gun barrel.

Canopy—The see-through cover over an airplane cockpit.

Casualty—A person wounded or killed, especially in battle.

Ceiling—The maximum altitude at which aircraft should normally fly.

Cockpit—The space where the pilot and co-pilot sit in an aircraft.

Commercial—Profit-making.

Console—A panel or cabinet on which are mounted dials and switches, used to control electrical or mechanical devices.

Converging—Moving toward each other or toward the same point.

Cylinder—An enclosed chamber in which force is exerted on the piston of an engine.

Debris (de-BREE)—The remains of something destroyed.

Detect—To discover or determine the existence of something.

Diameter—The length of a straight line through the center of an object such as a rotor.

Downwash—Air waves produced by the rotor blades of a helicopter.

Drag—Air resistance acting on a helicopter while it is in the air, opposite to the direction the helicopter is moving.

Electronics—The science that deals with the behavior of electrons in vacuums and gases, and with the use of vacuum tubes, transistors, and other advanced equipment.

Escort—Armed helicopters which accompany transports or other aircraft and protect against enemy attacks.

Evacuate—To remove from a military zone or dangerous area.

Flare—A bright burst of light which lasts only a short time.

Frequency—A measurement of electromagnetic waves, used in radio and television transmission.

Frigate (FRI-git)—A United States warship of 5,000 to 7,000 tons that is smaller than a cruiser and larger than a destroyer.

Fuselage (FEW-suh-lahj)—The main body of the helicopter or airplane.

Grenade—A small bomb with a fuse, thrown by hand or fired from a rifle.

Gunship—An armed helicopter that escorts unarmed troop transports.

Hoist—To lift or pull up heavy things with a cable or crane.

Homing—Aiming directly at the heart of the target.

Horsepower—A unit for measuring the power of an engine.

Hover (HUV-er)—To stay in midair in one place.

Howitzer—A short cannon which fires shells in a curved path.

Hull—The frame or main body of a ship or aircraft that can land on water.

Hydraulic—Mechanical properties of water and other liquids in engineering.

Intercept—To stop or interrupt the progress or course of.

Jam—To block or obstruct, as with radio communications.

Laser—Light Amplification by Simulated Emission of Radiation; a device that generates an intense and highly concentrated beam of light.

Lift—The force needed to overcome weight and raise it off the ground.

Maneuverable—Able to be controlled expertly and skillfully.

Militia (mi-LISH-uh)—Part of the organized armed forces of a country.

Mines—Underwater bombs.

Minigun—A rotating-barrel machine gun with a rapid-fire mechanism.

Mobile—Able to be moved or transported quickly and easily.

Payload—The bomb or cargo load of an aircraft.

Piston engine—An engine powered by pistons; pistons are solid metal pieces in the cylinder moved by a rod which is connected to the crankshaft; the movement of the pistons is sent on to the crankshaft.

Pitch angle—The angle between the rotor blade and main rotor hub which produces lift in a helicopter.

Plexiglas—A clear, lightweight substance used as a cockpit cover for airplanes.

Pods—Containers.

Radar—A device that determines location and distance of objects by ultra-high frequency radio waves.

Range—A specific distance.

Reconnaissance—The art of obtaining information about an enemy area; a survey or examination.

Retardant—Tending to slow down, delay, or hold back.

Retractable—Able to be drawn up under the fuselage of the helicopter.

Rotor—The rotating blades of the helicopter.

Round—A unit of ammunition; one shot.

Rudder—A device used to steer a helicopter.

Satellite—A man-made object put into orbit around the earth, the sun, or some other heavenly body.

Sensor—A device that responds to heat, light, or motion and then triggers a control.

Skid—A runner used in place of a wheel on an aircraft landing gear.

Sonar—Used in detecting submarines; transmits high-frequency sound waves in water and registers vibrations reflected back from an object.

Squadron—A unit of military flight formation.

Stowage—The storage of equipment or goods.

Surveillance—Close watch kept over a person or group.

Tandem—Seated or placed one behind the other.

Torque (TORK)—The tendency of the rotor blades to swing and twist the helicopter around.

Transmission—Part of the helicopter which transmits force from the engine to the rotors.

Turbine (TER-byn)—An engine driven by the pressure of steam, water, or air against the curved blades of a wheel or set of wheels.

Turbojet—A jet engine in which the energy of the jet operates a turbine which in turn operates an air compressor.

Turboshaft—A jet engine that uses the blast of expanding gases to spin a turbine that cranks a powershaft; the shaft turns the rotor of the helicopter though a series of gears.

Turret—A clear, Plexiglas half-globe in which guns are mounted.

Utility—The ability of an aircraft to serve in different jobs or positions; designed for general use.